Published by Creative Education
P.O. Box 227, Mankato, Minnesota 56002
Creative Education is an imprint of The Creative Company

Design by Stephanie Blumenthal; Production by The Design Lab
Printed in the United States of America

Photographs by CLEO Photography, Dennis Frates, Image Finders (Jim Baron, Alan Chapman,
Mark E. Gibson, Bruce Leighty, Michael Lustbader, William Manning, Mark & Sue Werner, Joanne
Williams), iStockphotos.com (AFP), JLM Visuals (Burton A. Amundson, J.C. Cokendolpher, Charlie
Crangle, Richard P. Jacobs, Breck P. Kent, Lowell R. Laudon, John Minnich, Marypat Zitzer), George
Robbins, Tom Stack & Associates (Jeff Foott, Milton Rand, Allen B. Smith, Greg Vaughn)

Library of Congress Cataloging-in-Publication Data
Frisch, Aaron.
Lakes / by Aaron Frisch.
p. cm. — (Our world)
Includes index.
ISBN 978-1-58341-571-9
1. Lake ecology—Juvenile literature. 2. Lakes—Juvenile literature. I. Title
QH541.5.L3F75 2008   577.63—dc22   2006102989

First edition
2 4 6 8 9 7 5 3 1

OUR WORLD

L
A
K
E
S

Aaron Frisch

A lake is a circle of water that has land all around it. There are lakes all over the world. A very little lake is called a pond. A very big lake might be called a sea.

The water in lakes is usually still. It does not move like the water in a river does. Water in the ocean has salt in it. But the water in most lakes does not.

Lakes come in lots of different sizes

Most lakes were made by glaciers *(GLAY-sherz)*. Glaciers are like mountains of ice. They move slowly. When they move, they make holes in the ground. Some of the holes fill up with water. They become lakes.

*Glaciers cut
into the ground*

People can make lakes, too. People build **dams** in rivers. Sometimes this makes a lake called a reservoir (*REZ-erv-war*). People get water for drinking from reservoirs.

Dams block water for people to use

*Lakes have algae
and lily pads*

Plants grow in lakes. Many lakes have algae *(AL-jee).* Algae are tiny green plants. They grow on top of the water. Many lakes have weeds and lily pads.

Big and small animals live in lakes

Lots of animals live in lakes. Turtles and frogs live in lakes. Many kinds of fish live there, too. Ducks swim on lakes. So do animals like **muskrats**. In Africa, big animals like hippos live in lakes.

Many people like to ride in boats on lakes. Other people like to swim in lakes. In the winter, some lakes get cold and freeze. They are covered in ice. People can make holes in the ice and go fishing!

*Lakes in cold
places can freeze*

Lakes do not last forever. Dirt and plant parts can fill up a lake. Then the lake stops being a lake. It becomes a **swamp** instead. This takes a long time. It can take 10,000 years!

Swamps have more weeds than lakes do

People can hurt lakes. If they dump dirty things into lakes, the lakes become **polluted** (*puh-LOO-tid*). Plants and fish might die. The lakes become less pretty, too. People need to help keep lakes clean!

Pollution makes water look dirty

Find a pointy rock as big as your hand. Drag the rock across some dirt. The rock is like a glacier. It makes a hole in the ground. Now pour some water into the hole to make a little lake. Slowly drop the dirt you scooped out back into the hole. Your lake will become muddy, like a swamp.

GLOSSARY

dams—walls that people build to block or change rivers

muskrats—furry little animals that like to swim

polluted—dirty or filled with things that are not healthy

swamp—a wild place that is muddy and has a little bit
of water

LEARN MORE ABOUT LAKES

Enchanted Learning
http://www.enchantedlearning.
com/biomes/pond/pondlife.shtml
This site has lots of pictures of pond animals.

Missouri Botanical Garden
http://www.mbgnet.net/fresh/
lakes/index.htm
This site has all kinds of facts about lakes.